# Maisie and the Puffer

# Maisie and the Puffer

*Author and illustrator*  Aileen Paterson

THE AMAISING PUBLISHING HOUSE LTD

This book is dedicated to the noble puffer, S.L. VIC 32, and her owners, Nick and Rachel Walker, Crinan Ferry, Lochgilphead. They restored her and run her as a holiday puffer to a standard which has gained Mrs McKitty's gold seal of approval! Also included in this dedication are Alice and Robert Walker, Rose, Nicky and Simon, and Muriel and Angus Robertson of Dumbarton. (Last but not least, it is my small tribute to Neil Munro and his immortal Para Handy).

© Aileen Paterson

First Published in 1992 by The Amaising Publishing House Ltd, reprinted 1994, 1997, 1999.

This edition published in 2001 by:
**Glowworm Books Ltd**, Unit 7, Greendykes Industrial Estate, Broxburn, West Lothian, EH52 6PG, Scotland.

*Telephone:* 01506-857570
*Fax:* 01506-858100
*URL:* http://www.glowwormbooks.co.uk

ISBN 1 871512 33 6

Printed and bound by Scotprint

Designed by Mark Blackadder

Reprint Code    10    9    8    7    6    5

**Other Maisie titles in the Series:**

Maisie Mackenzie is a wee tabby kitten. Her Daddy is an explorer cat and often away travelling in far foreign lands, so Maisie stays with her Granny in Edinburgh. They live in a flat in Morningside Mansions, next door to Mrs McKitty — the most pernickety, panloaf pussycat in the whole of Scotland. Maisie and her friends have to mind their Ps and Qs when Mrs McKitty is about. Woe betide any kitten who drops a sweetie wrapper on the stairs!

Mrs McKitty is related to the Siamese families of Ravelston Dykes, and the MacSporrans of Lady Road — *and* the McSwankies of Belgrave Mews! There is nothing she likes better than to invite Granny in for coffee so she can tell her all the latest news about her family. There is always so much news, and so many photographs of Mrs McKitty's marvellous relatives to see, that poor Granny can never get a word in edgeways about the Mackenzie family.

But one day, Granny got her chance to show off. The postie brought her a letter from her cousin Sandy in Ardrishaig. Granny was very proud of Sandy. He was a seafaring cat who had been all over the world and many other places. Now he was the captain of his very own boat — *The Nippy Sweetie*. Granny had never seen *The Nippy Sweetie*, but Sandy said she was the smartest steamboat ever to put to sea. When Mrs McKitty popped in that morning, it was Granny who had exciting family news for *her* — Sandy had invited them all, including Mrs McKitty and her budgie Billy, to come for a cruising holiday!

"A CRUISE! Oh, Blissykins!" cried Mrs McKitty. "I *love* cruising. The sun, the sea, the food, the cocktail parties and deck games. Tell your cousin we should be delighted to accept." Granny wrote back at once to say they would all love to come, and that they would be arriving in Ardrishaig on the one o'clock bus the following Friday.

There was a tremendous whirl of activity in both flats that
week. While Granny washed and ironed, Maisie was busy writing
a letter . . .

JAPAN

to Maisie
from Daddy
X

Dear Daddy, Thank you for
the postcard from Japan
with the fat cat on it. I hope
you are fine. Granny is fine
and I am fine. We have
great news! We are going
for a ~~croose~~ cruise on
Uncle Sandy's boat. Granny
says he is the bravest
captain in the world. Mrs
McKitty and Billy are
coming with us.
Lots of love,
maisie xx

Mrs McKitty was busy too. She bought some very smart holiday outfits by Muriel de Morningside, and telephoned all her friends and family with the news of the cruise. Meanwhile Billy sat on his swing and practised being a seagoing budgie.

"Avast me hearties! Shiver me timbers, I'm a salty son of a sea parrot," he chirruped, bashing his bell with glee. "Yo, Ho, Ho and a bottle of Irn Bru!"

At last it was Friday, and the four holidaymakers set off on the bus bound for the west coast of Scotland. Soon they would be aboard *The Nippy Sweetie*, having a wonderful time and lots of surprises.

(There were quite a few in store . . . )

Granny's first surprise was that there was no sign of Sandy when they got off the bus, but a wee brown cat with a wheelbarrow was waiting.

"Hello Mrs Mackenzie," he cried. "Nice to see you all. The Captain's just bringing the boat down the canal, so he sent me to fetch you and your luggage. I'm Doogie MacDoogall, First Mate on *The Nippy Sweetie*."

Mrs McKitty was surprised to hear that. *First Mate!* She couldn't help noticing Doogie's oily paws and the hole in his jersey! She had been expecting an officer cat in a white uniform with brass buttons to greet them. ''Gracious me,'' she remarked to Billy as they followed the wheelbarrow. ''Standards are fairly slipping in this part of Scotland. How lucky we are to live in Edinburgh.''

Doogie led them across the road and along the path beside the Crinan Canal. There they got their first sight of *The Nippy Sweetie!* A black boat, blowing clouds of smoke from a sooty funnel as she edged her way through the lock and into the Canal Basin. Maisie watched in wonder as her Uncle Sandy squeezed his big boat through the narrow space and steered towards them.

''Captain!'' shouted Doogie. ''Your visitors are here.'' A stripey grey cat, wearing a captain's cap, stuck his head out of the wheelhouse and waved.

''By Chove,'' he cried in a soft Highland accent. ''It's yourself, Isabella, and Maisie too. And you will be Mrs McKitty, and himself is your wee bird. Welcome! Wait till we tie up, and Doogie will be getting you aboard.'' But Maisie couldn't wait another minute. With one bound, she leapt on to the deck ahead of the others and joined her uncle on his fine big boat.

Maisie was thrilled to bits but, as the others followed Doogie across the gangplank, Granny was in for another surprise. In fact, it was more like a shock! One glance told her that this was NOT a posh cruise ship!

IT WAS NOTHING BUT A *PUFFER* — A COMMON LITTLE CARGO BOAT!

There would be no cocktail parties for Mrs McKitty, nor deck games. The deck was covered with egg boxes, bags of potatoes and cement, and a crate of chickens. There was even an old wardrobe and a cooker!! She could not bear to look at her friend as they followed Doogie below to the saloon . . .

The Captain came in behind them, with Maisie and a grimy cat wearing an oily bunnet and a boiler suit, whom he introduced as his Chief Engineer — Jake McCraik from Partick.

"Sit yourselves down," cried Captain Sandy. "Doogie and Jake will make us a nice cup of tea. We've a grand modern kitchen, by the by. My, Isabella, but I'm that pleased to see you all. We could do with a helping paw here on *The Nippy Sweetie.* Our cook, Murdo, is away to Australia to visit his Auntie Senga.

Doogie took on the cooking, but he's for no use at all, at all.
We've had nothing but corned beef sandwiches and haddocks fried
in engine oil, for WEEKS!''

Poor Granny groaned, and there was a low growling noise
from the direction of Mrs McKitty's chair, but Captain Sandy
didn't hear. Someone was calling to him from the quayside. The
crew of the puffer jumped up and made for the stairs.

''Excuse us for a minute,'' beamed Uncle Sandy. ''A sailor's
work is never done. We've a delivery of fuel to get on board.
It won't take long, whateffer. Then it's full steam ahead for your
cruise 'doon the watter'.''

Mrs McKitty watched the crew disappear up on deck, then
she drew herself up to her full height. Maisie gulped as she
marched past . . . Mrs McKitty's face was PURPLE with fury!

''DOON THE WATTER, indeed!'' she yowled. ''UP THE
CREEK is more like it. This boat should be declared a disaster
area. Just come and look at THIS!''

Maisie and Granny followed her to the doorway leading to

the boat's 'grand modern kitchen'. Granny gave another groan
. . . a loud one this time. The kitchen, awash with unwashed
dishes and corned beef tins, looked like a storm at sea!

"Follow me!" growled Mrs McKitty. "It's time we had a
few words with your cousin. I'll give him 'haddocks fried in
engine oil'."

She marched ahead of Granny and Maisie, straight up to the
top of the deck where Jake was to be seen. None of them noticed
a coal lorry on the quay which was backed up against the side of
the boat. Just as Mrs McKitty was about to demand to see the
Captain, there was a loud rumbling noise, and a huge load of coal
erupted out of the back of the lorry, cascading onto the deck.

Most of it shot down into the coal hole, but a great deal flew sideways, scattering dust and fragments everywhere. Mrs McKitty's lovely white suit was ruined, and Billy the budgie had changed in the twinkling of an eye from a blue bird to a blackbird! There was a moment's silence, then Mrs McKitty gave a screech which nearly blew Jake's bunnet off!

"THIS IS THE LAST STRAW! THIS PUTS THE TIN LID ON IT!" With that she swept up Billy's cage and disappeared below decks. Granny was shattered. Her dreams of treating Mrs McKitty to a splendid cruise on her cousin's smart steamboat had gone up in smoke and coal dust. Furthermore, she was black affronted. What must Mrs McKitty be thinking of the Mackenzie family?

"Cheer up," said the Captain. "It was chust a mishap . . . chust a wee drop of coal. Soap and water will soon put everything right."

Granny covered her face with her paws. It would take more than soap and water to put this disaster right. She knew Mrs McKitty would be heading back to Edinburgh on the very next bus.

Everything went quiet. There was a hushed silence as they waited for Mrs McKitty to come back. Maisie held Granny's paw. Suddenly there were loud pawsteps, and Mrs McKitty bounded up the narrow stairs!

Everyone stared in astonishment when they saw her. She had washed off every trace of coal dust, but she was no longer dressed in one of Muriel de Morningside's snappy outfits. Instead, she had on a boiler suit and a bunnet!

*Mrs McKitty was dressed for ACTION!!*

"Marjorie!" gasped Granny. "I . . . I thought you were packing up to go home . . . "

"GO HOME!? Not I!" cried Mrs McKitty. "I am one of the McKittys of Morningside, and a McKitty never admits defeat! I am taking charge of this boat till further notice. It needs a firm paw . . . and a good clean! I've made a list of all the jobs to be done, and we are not leaving harbour till they are done."

The crew of *The Nippy Sweetie* were staggered.

"Chust a minute," stammered Captain Sandy. "This is mutiny . . . MUTINY! I'm in charge of this puffer . . . "

Granny interrupted him . . .

"Mrs McKitty is quite right, Sandy. This boat is a disgrace. And, if you don't do what she says, we will all leave and you won't get a good home-cooked dinner tonight!"

The captain remembered Doogie's menu, and after one look at the mighty Mrs McKitty, he gave in. He told Jake and Doogie to do what she told them to do, then he locked himself in his cabin.

For the next two hours, there was a hurlyburly of rubbing, scrubbing, washing and polishing. Mrs McKitty was enjoying herself thoroughly, getting everything shipshape and bossing her crew. Jake and Doogie were sent off to the kitchen to clean it till it sparkled. They also took all the rubbish, including the last of the dreaded corned beef, and emptied it into the harbour dustbin.

Even Billy had a shower and spring-cleaned his cage. When Maisie got a moment to spare, she tiptoed off to have a word with Uncle Sandy. She gave him some good advice about how to get on the right side of Mrs McKitty.

"My, but you are the clever kitten," said her uncle. "Now, chust tell your Granny to go along to Haggis Angus at The Puffer Provision Stores, and order whateffer she needs for the cruise. Angus will put it on my account. Thank you, Maisie."

That evening, the puffer was perfumed with the scent of furniture polish and delicious smells from the kitchen. The table was set, and the candles were lit. In his cabin, the Captain inspected his crew, who were dressed up in their best.

"I'm fair proud of you, lads," he told them. "You look as smart as any of the nobs parading along Piccadilly or Princes Street. Well done!"

When Maisie rang the ship's bell to announce that dinner was served, they stepped out. The Captain made a bow, then presented Mrs McKitty and Granny each with a bouquet of flowers.

"This is chust a wee thank you from me and the crew. You've made *The Nippy Sweetie* into the smartest cruise boat in Scotland."

Granny and Mrs McKitty were delighted. Peace and joy settled on the puffer, and as they sat down to eat Scotch Broth, mince and tatties, rhubarb tart and custard, the Captain sighed happily . . . "By Chove — is this not sublime?"

Early next morning their week's cruise began. *The Nippy Sweetie* slipped out of Ardrishaig Harbour into Loch Fyne, and headed for Tarbert. It was a fine morning, and Doogie cleared a space on the deck and set up a table and sun brolly for Mrs

McKitty. Down below in the kitchen, Granny sang as she stirred the porridge, and Jake whistled as he shovelled coal into the boiler. Maisie danced a Sailor's Hornpipe as she hung the washing out to dry. Billy the budgie was feeling chirpy too . . . Captain Sandy had found him a very important job. He was up on the mast, keeping a look-out for dangers to shipping, like sharks and whales and icebergs!

When they reached Tarbert that afternoon, the crew went off to deliver their cargo. The wardrobe and cooker went off to The Oorain Guest House, the eggs and potatoes to the Tarbert Tearoom, and the chickens and cement to a croft on the hill. Granny, Maisie and Mrs McKitty walked around the bonny harbour, and visited the shops and bought presents and postcards for their families and friends. When they got back to the boat, a

surprise awaited them. The crew had set the table and prepared dinner all by themselves . . . Fish and Chips and Pickled Onions from The Loch Fyne Fish Bar! Delicious!

As the holiday went on, and they steamed up and down the lochs around the Kyles of Bute they began to have the time of their lives. They went fishing, and picking blaeberries, and Maisie went paddling and met an otter. They had a day in Rothesay, seeing the sights, eating ice cream, and having a High Tea. Mrs McKitty enjoyed getting dressed up in her finery, and strolling under the palm trees by the bay.

They did some daft things too . . . like the day Maisie and
Jake painted 'The Cats of Bute'! They weren't *real* cats, of course.
Just two big stones standing on the hillside overlooking Loch
Riddon. Jake said they reminded him of the McStookie sisters,
two cats he used to take to the dancing in Glasgow, so Captain
Sandy suggested that he take a break from the stoking and paint
them to look like Peggy and Sadie McStookie. Maisie and Jake
made a lovely job of painting 'The Cats of Bute' . . . and now
they are a real tourist attraction!

They had another Daft Day picnicking in the pouring rain.
When they arrived at the beach it was hot and sunny but they
were plagued by midgies. Suddenly the weather changed. Dark
clouds gathered and it began to rain cats and dogs. What with the
millions of midgies and then the downpour Granny suggested they
should pack up.

"Not a bit of it, it's only a shower," said Mrs McKitty
pulling on her rainhat and putting the kettle on the fire.

"How did you enjoy the picnic, Maisie?" asked Uncle Sandy when they got back aboard.

"It was great, Uncle Sandy. Mrs McKitty had fun too — she even said the food was delicious although the tea was smoky and our egg sandwiches were soggy. I've never seen her in such a good mood. She's never like this at home. There must be a kind of magic in the air down here."

"You are quite right, Maisie," said her uncle, smiling. "There is a magic about this part of the world. When Mrs McKitty came aboard, she was a wee bit toffee-nosed, and now she is as nice as ninepence! My Granny used to say it was all due to the fairyfolk who live hereabouts, and you'll find the magic stays with you for quite a while after you get home."

At last their magical week came to an end. On their last night aboard *The Nippy Sweetie*, they had a Farewell Party. Captain Sandy and the crew laid on a lovely supper . . . salmon sandwiches, chocolate biscuits, cake and jelly, and budgie treats for Billy! After supper, they cleared the floor and danced reels and jigs till dawn!

When they were back home in Edinburgh, Mrs McKitty invited Granny and Maisie in for coffee and lemonade, to see her holiday snaps. Maisie couldn't help smiling as she looked at them. They were all of Mrs McKitty in her smart outfits, standing in front of a *luxury yacht!* . . . You wouldn't have known she had been on a puffer cruise *at all!*

But there was still some of the magic of their holiday about, in Mrs McKitty's kitchen, when she had a word with Granny . . .

"Thank you so much for inviting me to go on our cruise," she said. "*Do* send Captain Mackenzie my felicitations! I'm feeling so well . . . just like a new cat, and Billy is singing like a lintie. Shall we go back next summer?"

Granny and Maisie glowed with joy. They went home and looked at their own holiday snaps, and felt so proud of Uncle Sandy, and his crew, who had given them such a good time, and the wonderful *Nippy Sweetie*, which had turned into the smartest cruise puffer ever to sail 'doon the watter'!

What did we do on *The Nippy Sweetie*,
What did we do on *The Nippy Sweetie*,
What did we do on *The Nippy Sweetie*,
Early in the morning.

Hooray and up she rises,
Hooray and up she rises,
Hooray and up she rises,
Early in the morning.

Polished the bell and peeled the tatties,
Scrubbed the deck, and washed the dishes,
Painted the funnel and caught three fishes,
Early in the morning.

Hooray and up she rises,
Hooray and up she rises,
Hooray and up she rises,
Early in the morning.

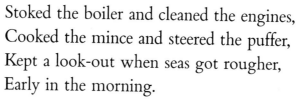

Stoked the boiler and cleaned the engines,
Cooked the mince and steered the puffer,
Kept a look-out when seas got rougher,
Early in the morning.

Hooray and up she rises,
Hooray and up she rises,
Hooray and up she rises,
Early in the morning.

That's what we did on *The Nippy Sweetie*,
That's what we did on *The Nippy Sweetie*,
That's what we did on *The Nippy Sweetie*,
Early in the morning.

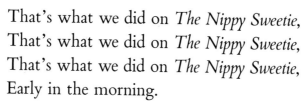

Hooray and up she rises,
Hooray and up she rises,
Hooray and up she rises,
Early in the morning.

## Glossary

| | |
|---|---|
| *Ardrishaig* | village on Loch Fyne, beside the south end of Crinan Canal |
| *black affronted* | embarrassed |
| *blaeberries* | bilberries |
| *bunnet* | a flat cap |
| *'doon the watter'* | 'down the water' usually taken to mean the Firth of Clyde |
| *hornpipe* | a sailor's dance |
| *Irn Bru* | our other national drink |
| *Kyles of Bute* | stretch of sea water round Bute |
| *lintie* | a linnet |
| *Morningside/Ravelston Dykes, etc* | select Edinburgh suburbs |
| *Nippy Sweetie* | various meanings including — 'a cough drop' |
| *nob* | a superior person |
| *panloaf* | affected way of speaking |
| *pernickety* | fussy |
| *puffer* | a small sturdy steam coastal boat used to carry cargo |
| *Scotch Broth* | soup made with barley and vegetables |
| *tatties* | potatoes |
| *toffee-nosed* | snobbish |